PATRICK
McGRATH

THE ANGEL
AND OTHER STORIES

PENGUIN BOOKS

PENGUIN BOOKS

Published by the Penguin Group. Penguin Books Ltd, 27 Wrights Lane, London
W8 5TZ, England. Penguin Books USA Inc., 375 Hudson Street, New York, New
York 10014, USA. Penguin Books Australia Ltd, Ringwood, Victoria, Australia.
Penguin Books Canada Ltd, 10 Alcorn Avenue, Toronto, Ontario, Canada M4V 3B2.
Penguin Books (NZ) Ltd, 182–190 Wairau Road, Auckland 10, New Zealand ·
Penguin Books Ltd, Registered Offices: Harmondsworth, Middlesex, England ·
These stories have been taken from *Blood and Water* by Patrick McGrath,
first published in the USA by Poseidon Press, a division of Simon and
Schuster, Inc. in 1988 and published by Penguin Books in 1989. This edition
published 1995 · Copyright © Patrick McGrath, 1988. All rights reserved · The
moral right of the author has been asserted · Filmset by Datix International
Limited, Bungay, Suffolk. Printed in England by Clays Ltd, St Ives plc · Except
in the United States of America, this book is sold subject to the condition
that it shall not, by way of trade or otherwise, be lent, re-sold, hired out,
or otherwise circulated without the publisher's prior consent in any form of
binding or cover other than that in which it is published and without a similar
condition including this condition being imposed on the subsequent purchaser ·
10 9 8 7 6 5 4 3 2 1

CONTENTS

The Angel

You know the Bowery, I presume? It was on the Bowery that I first caught a glimpse of Harry Talboys. I was a writer in those days, and I lived in a five-story walk-up by the men's shelter. I didn't realize at the time that Harry Talboys lived in the same building, though of course I was familiar with the powerful smell of incense that contaminated the lower floors. It was high summer when I met him, high summer in Manhattan, when liquid heat settles on the body of the city like an incubus, and one's whole activity devolves to a languid commerce of flesh and fluids, the ingestion and excretion of the one by the other, and all sane organisms quite simply estivate. I was certainly estivating; I rose late in the day, and after certain minimal ritualistic gestures of the writerly kind made my way to the liquor store. It was on one of these errands, on a garbage-strewn and urine-pungent sidewalk, beneath a blazing sun, and slimed in my own sweat, that I first encountered Harry Talboys.

He was making stately progress down the Bowery with a cane. Let me describe him: a tall, thin figure in a seersucker suit the grubbiness of which, the fraying cuffs, the cigarette burns and faded reddish wine stain on the crotch could not altogether disguise the quality of the fabric and the elegance of the cut. Very erect, very tall, very slow, on his head a Panama hat; and his face a veritable atlas of human experience, 1 the nose a great hooked bone of a thing projecting like the prow of a ship, and the mouth – well, the mouth had foundered somewhat, but the old man animated it with lipstick! He must have been at least eighty. His shirt collar was not clean, and he wore a silk tie of some pastel shade – pale lilac or mauve, I seem to remember; and in his buttonhole a fresh white lily. (I never saw Harry Talboys without a fresh flower in his buttonhole.) And as I say, he was making his way down the Bowery, and the men from the men's shelter drinking at the corner of Third Street greeted him warmly. 'Hey, Harry!' they called; 'Yo, Harry!' and he moved through them with all the graceful condescension of royalty, briefly lifting his Panama to reveal a liver-spotted skull devoid of all but a last few wisps of snow-white hair. Watching this performance I was much taken with the dignity of the old fellow, and with his lipstick. Was there, I asked myself, a story here?

Our friendship began well: he asked me into his apartment for a drink. Such a hot day, he said, hanging up his Panama in the hallway and leaning his stick in the corner; productive activity, he said, was quite out of the question. His accent, to my surprise, was old Boston. (I'm from the North End myself.) The odor of incense was strong, and so was the perfume he wore. He was very liberally scented and smelled, in fact, like an old lady, but there was, I detected it even then, something unpleasant about it, a nuance, a suggestion of overripeness in the bouquet.

Are you familiar with the apartments of the Lower East Side? Designed essentially as holding tanks for wage laborers, they do not err on the side of expansiveness. We entered Harry's living room. Crowded bookshelves, a pair of deep seedy armchairs that faced windows with a clear prospect north to the Chrysler Building, and between the windows, on a rounded, slender-stemmed table of varnished black wood, a vase full of lilies. Directly above the lilies, and between the windows, hung a large crucifix, the body of the Saviour pinned to a cross of white ivory with nailheads of mother-of pearl. Hanging from the ceiling in the far corner of the room, on a length of copper chain, was the censer whence the fumes emanated. No air conditioner, no fan. There was, however, ice in the kitchen, and Harry made us each a large gin-and-tonic. Then he lowered himself stiffly toward an armchair, the final stage of this operation being a sort of abandoned plunge followed by a long sigh. 'Cigarettes,' he murmured, rummaging through the pockets of his jacket.

'You have no cats,' I said.

'Dreadful creatures,' he said. 'Can't abide them. Your very good health, Bernard Finnegan!'

We drank. He asked me about my writing. I began to explain, but he quickly lost interest. His gaze shifted to the window, to the glittering blade that the Chrysler Building becomes in the shimmering blue heat of certain summer days. His books impressed me. A good many classical authors – Petronius was represented, Apuleius and Lactantius, and certain of the early Christian writers, Bede and Augustine among others. When I rose to leave, he asked me for my telephone number. Would I, he wondered, have a drink with him again? Yes, I said, with pleasure.

'Gin?'

The censer was, as before, smoldering gently on its chain. It reminded me of my childhood, of chapels and churches in which I had fidgeted through innumerable interminable Masses. Harry's perfume, slightly rotten though it was, one grew accustomed to; not the incense. The stink of it was apparent as soon as one entered the building. I asked him why he burned it.

'Does it disturb you?' he said. He was slicing a lemon on the kitchen counter, very slowly. I was in the other room. The Chrysler Building was glowing in the dusk, and there were red streaks to the west, over the Hudson.

'It makes me feel like a schoolboy.'

He looked at me carefully then, those watery blue eyes of his fixing me like a pair of headlights. 'Are you a Catholic?' he said.

'Lapsed.'

'I too.'

He sighed. He became preoccupied. He appeared to be pondering our common connection to the Roman faith. 'When I was a young man,' he said, when we were settled in our armchairs, 'I called myself a Catholic but I lived like a pagan. Oh, I could drink in those days, Bernard! I could drink till dawn. Today, as you see, after one gin I become' – here he smiled with gentle irony – 'desperately befuddled. But then! I was happy with my gods, like the ancients. Do you know what we thought the body was, Bernard, back in the Twenties? A temple in which there was nothing unclean. A shrine, to be adorned for the ritual of love! We lived for the moment, Bernard – the purpose of life was to express yourself, and if you were unhappy that was because you were maladjusted, and if you were maladjusted it was because you were repressed. We were excitable, you see, and if there was one thing we would not tolerate' – he turned toward me in his armchair – 'it was boredom! Dullness! Anathema!' He gazed off into the night. There was a silence.

'Go on,' I said.

'It didn't last. I remember coming back to New York in 1929 . . . My friends all seemed to be dead, or married, or alcoholic . . .' Another pause. 'I don't suppose you know the *Rhapsody in Blue*?' He hummed the opening bars, and there was suddenly a tone, in the thickening and aromatic dusk, of intense melancholy, rendered all the more poignant by the slow, faltering cadence of the old man's melody. He said little more that evening, and when I rose to leave he was distant and abstracted. He did apologize, though, for being 'such a wretched host'.

The summer progressed. In a gin-blurred heat haze we slipped into August. I spent two or three hours a day at my table and told myself I was working. In fact I made several verbal sketches of Harry Talboys; to what use I would put them I had no clear idea at the time.

The thunderstorms began – brief showers of intense rain, with lightning and thunder, which did nothing to disturb the pall of stale heat that clung to the stinking city. They ended as suddenly as they began, and left the streets still steaming and fetid. It occurred to me that I should more actively prompt Harry to reminisce. I wondered if, between us, we might not produce a memoir of the Twenties. We would call it *An Old Man Remembers the Jazz Age*, or something of the sort; lavishly illustrated with photographs from the period, it would stand as an expressive personal document of modern America in the innocent exuberance of its golden youth. The more I thought about it, the surer I felt that such a book was needed. I mentioned the idea to Harry when next I saw him. 'I knew an angel once,' he murmured. 'That was in the Twenties.'

It was, they said, the hottest summer in thirty years, and there was a distinct possibility that the garbage men would go on strike. A rather grisly murder occurred in an abandoned building over on Avenue C; the body was mutilated and drained of all its blood. The *New York Post* suggested that a vampire was on the loose. My own habits became increasingly nocturnal, and my productivity declined still further. I did manage to spend one afternoon in the public library looking at material from the Twenties, and made up a list of questions to put to Harry, questions which I hoped would release a rich flow of anecdotes. I felt like a prospector: if only, I thought, I could sink my probe with enough precision, up would gush the stuff to make us both some real money. The times were right, I became more certain than ever, for *An Old Man Remembers the Jazz Age*.

But Harry was harder to draw out than I'd anticipated. When next I broached the topic – it was a Friday evening, and the sunset was gorgeous – he spoke again of his angel.

He was relaxed and affable, I remember, and I humored him. 'You mean metaphorically he was an angel, Harry,' I said. 'You mean he was a very good man.'

'Oh, no,' said Harry, turning toward me. 'No, he was not a good man at all!' The armchairs were, as usual, facing the windows, angled only slightly toward each other, so we sat as if piloting some great craft into the darkling sky. 'But he was a real angel, absolutely authentic.'

'Who was he, Harry?'

'His name,' said Harry, 'was Anson Havershaw.' He sat forward and peered at me. 'You do want to hear the story?' he said. 'I should hate to bore you.'

When was it, precisely, that I began to take Harry's angel seriously? I suppose there was something in the tale that caught my imagination immediately. He described to me how, as a very young man, and fresh from Harvard, he had glimpsed across the floor of an elegant New York speakeasy a man who bore a striking resemblance to himself. 'An uncanny physical likeness,' said Harry. 'Perfectly extraordinary.' He had lost sight of the man, and spent an hour looking for him, without success. He returned to the speakeasy night after night; a week later he saw him again. He introduced himself. The other was Anson Havershaw, a wealthy and sophisticated young dandy, 'a much more polished character than I,' said Harry, 'and he recognized the similarity between us at once; it amused him. He asked me to lunch with him the following day at the Biltmore, and said that we should become friends.'

All light had faded from the sky by this point. There was a

long pause. 'Well, we did become friends,' said Harry at last, 'very good friends indeed. Oh, enough, Bernard!' He was sitting with one long leg crossed over the other, ankles sockless, his left hand clutching his right shoulder and his gaze fixed on the distant spire, which glittered in the darkness like a dagger. All the tension, all the vitality seemed suddenly to drain out of him. He sat there deflated and exhausted. The room was by this time full of shadows, and Harry was lumped in his armchair like a corpse. The exertion involved in his flight of memory seemed to have sharpened the foul smell that clung to him, for the perfume could no longer mask it at all. I moved quietly to the door. 'Call me,' I said, 'when you want to continue.' A hand flapped wearily from the arm of the chair. I left him there, alone in the shadows.

'It was some weeks later, when we were on terms of intimacy,' said Harry, when next we met, 'that Anson first invited me to his house. The front door was opened by his valet, an Englishman called Allardice. He showed me into Anson's dressing room and left me there.

'I settled myself to wait. After a few minutes Anson entered in a silk dressing gown of Chinese design, followed by Allardice. He greeted me warmly and asked if Allardice could get me anything; then he told me to talk to him while he dressed – or rather, while Allardice dressed him.'

A long pause here; Harry's fingers were kneading the arm of the chair. Then he began to speak quickly and warmly. 'Anson stepped up to the glass and slipped the gown from his shoulders; he stood there quite naked, with one foot advanced and turned very slightly outwards, and his fingers caught lightly on his hips. How tall and slender, and hairless he was! And white, Bernard, white as milk!'

Harry at this point sat up quite erect in his armchair and lifted a hand to sketch Anson's figure in the air before him. 'He had a neck like the stem of a flower,' he said softly, 'and narrow shoulders; and his chest was very flat, and very finely nippled, and merged imperceptibly into a belly punctuated by the merest suggestion of a navel. He stood before the glass and gazed at himself with all the impersonal admiration he might have expended on a piece of fine porcelain or a Ming vase, as though he knew he was quite beautiful, and suffered no impulse to humility on the point . . .'

Harry turned to me and held out his glass. There were pearls of perspiration on his forehead, and his smell was very bad. I gave him more gin. 'Then,' he went on, 'he had me come close and examine his body. There was a slight flap of skin midway between his hipbones, and believe me, Bernard, a flap is all it was; there was no knot to it. It was' – Harry groped for words – 'vestigial! It was . . . decorative!'

Silence in that gloom-laden and incense-reeking room.

'I asked him what he was. "I have not your nature," he said quite simply. "I am of the angels."'

Harry's gaze shifted back to the open window. 'The dressing proceeded,' he whispered, 'and when Anson looked upon his final perfection, Allardice came forward with a flower for his buttonhole – an orchid, I think it was; and then at last the hush and reverence were banished. "Come, Harry," he cried, and together we glided down the stairs, with Allardice, close behind, intent upon the flurry of instructions Anson was giving him with regard to the evening. I was, I suppose, utterly mystified, and utterly intoxicated by this time, for I followed him; I followed him like a shadow . . .'

Harry fell silent again. His hand was still lifted in the air, and trembling, as he stared out of the window. As for myself, I felt suddenly impatient of this talk. These, I said to myself, are nothing but the gin-fired fantasies of a maudlin old queen. I muttered some excuse and left; Harry barely noticed.

There comes a day, in the ripe maturity of late summer, when you first detect a suggestion of the season to come; often as subtle as a play of evening light against familiar bricks, or the drift of a few brown leaves descending, it signals imminent release from savage heat and intemperate growth. You anticipate cool, misty days, and a slow, comely decadence in the order of the natural. Such a day now dawned; and my pale northern soul, in its pale northern breast, quietly exulted as the earth slowly turned its face from the sun. This quickening of the spirit was accompanied, in my relationship with Harry, by disillusion and withdrawal. Oddly enough, though, I spoke of his angel to no one; it was as though I'd tucked it into some dark grotto of my brain, there to hold it secret and inviolate.

The murder victim of Avenue C, ran the prevailing theory, was a double-crosser involved in a major drug deal. The nastiness was presumed to be a warning to others not to make the same mistake. The garbage men went out on strike for three days, but a settlement was reached before things really began to go bad, and the trucks were soon rolling again – stinking ripely and clouded with insects, noxious monsters trumpeting and wheezing through the midnight streets. The one that serviced my block was called *The Pioneer*, and on the side of it was painted a covered wagon rumbling across some western prairie. When I found myself downwind of *The Pioneer*, I thought, unkindly, of Harry.

It was at around this time that I began to toy with the notion of a historical novel about heretics. I'd chanced upon a gnostic tale in which Satan, a great god, creates a human body and persuades a spirit called Arbal-Jesus to project his being into it for a few moments. Arbal-Jesus complies with Satan's seemingly innocent request, but once inside the body he finds himself trapped, and cannot escape. He screams in agony, but Satan only laughs; and then mocks his captive by sexually violating him. Arbal-Jesus' only consolation is that another spirit accompanies him in the body, and guarantees his release. That spirit is Death.

But then the brief taste of fall vanished, and the heat returned with greater ferocity than ever. On my way out one morning I met Harry. 'Bernard,' he said, 'why do I never see you now?' I felt guilty. He looked rather more seedy than usual; his jaw was stubbled with fine white hairs, and traces of dried blood adhered to his nostrils. His bony fingers clutched my arm. 'Come down this evening,' he said. 'I have gin.' Poor old man, I thought, lonely and shabby, scraping about in two rooms after all these years . . . why does he still cling to the raft?

I knocked on Harry's door around seven. All was as usual – the smells, the gin, the Chrysler Building rising like a jeweled spearhead against the sky, and upon Harry's wall the crucifix shining in the shadows of the fading day. Poor old Harry; I sensed immediately he wanted to continue with his story, but was holding back out of deference to me. I felt compelled to reopen the subject, though not simply out of courtesy to an old man's obsession. I had been thinking some more about this shadowy figure, the beautiful, decadent Anson Havershaw, he of the milk-white flesh and the non-existent navel, and about Harry's cryptic but no doubt carnal relationship with him. It was, I felt, a most bizarre fiction he had begun to weave about a man who, I presumed, had in fact actually existed, and indeed might still be alive.

So Harry began to talk. He described how Anson swept him into a summer of hectic and dazzling pleasures, of long nights, riotous and frenzied, when all of America seemed to be convulsed in a spasm of fevered gaiety, and the two of them had moved through the revels like a pair of gods, languid, elegant, twin souls presiding with heavy-lidded eyes over the nation's binge. That summer, the summer of 1925, Harry often found himself leaving Anson's house in the first light of dawn, still in evening clothes, and slipping into the welcome gloom of St Ignatius Loyola on Park Avenue. 'You wouldn't know it, Bernard,' he said; 'they tore it down in 1947. A lovely church, Gothic Revival; I miss it . . . at the early Mass it would be lit only by the dim, blood-red glow from the stained-glass windows, and by a pair of white candles that rose from gilded holders on either side of the altar and threw out a gorgeous, shimmering halo ... The priest I knew well, an ascetic young Jesuit; I remember how his pale face caught the candlelight as he turned to the congregation – the whole effect was so strangely beautiful, Bernard, if you had seen it you would understand the attraction Catholicism held for so many of us ... it was the emotional appeal, really; disciplined Christianity we found more difficult to embrace ...'

Harry rambled on in this vein for some minutes, his eyes on the spire and his fingers curled about his glass. My own thoughts drifted off down parallel tracks, lulled comfortably by his voice. As a raconteur Harry was slow and fastidious; he composed his sentences with scrupulous care and lingered indulgently over his more graceful phrases. 'I doubt I would have done well in business,' he was saying, inconsequentially; 'I just haven't the kidney for it. One needs strong nerves, and I was always much too effete. Anson used to say that the world was a brothel, and he was right, of course. So where is one to turn? I can tell you where I turned: straight into the arms of Mother Church!' He swallowed the rest of his gin. 'But that's another story, and forgive me, Bernard, I seem to be digressing again. All this happened so very long ago, you see, that I tend to confuse the order in which things occurred ...

'There are two questions, Bernard, that have to be addressed to an angel. One concerns his origins; the other, his purpose.'

·

At these words I began to pay active attention once more. This angel business was, of course, nonsense; but I had come to suspect that something rather fantastic, or even perverse, might lie behind it.

'About his origins I could learn almost nothing,' Harry continued. 'People said he arrived in New York during the last year of the first war; he had apparently been raised in Ireland by his mother, who was from Boston and had married into an obscure branch of the Havershaws of Cork, an eccentric family, so they said; but then, you see, well-born Europeans with cloudy origins have always been drifting into New York, and so long as their manners and their money are adequate – particularly the latter – they're admitted to society and no one's very bothered about where they've come from. We are, after all, a republic.'

Boston! At the mention of Boston an idea suddenly occurred to me. Harry was old Boston, this I knew, and I wondered whether this angel of his might be nothing more than an elaborate sexual disguise. Anson Havershaw, by this theory, was simply an alter ego, a detached figment of Harry's neurotic imagination, a double or other constructed as a sort of libidinal escape valve. In other words, Harry transcended his own guilty carnality by assuming at one remove the identity of an angel – this would explain the physical resemblance between the two, and the contradictory themes of hedonism and spirituality; what Catholic, after all, lapsed or otherwise, could ever believe the body was a temple in which nothing was unclean? I watched Harry smiling to himself, and his expression, in the twilight, and despite the patrician dignity of the nose, seemed suddenly silly, pathetic.

'And his purpose?' I said drily.

'Ah.' The pleasure slowly ebbed from his face, and he began to make an unpleasant sucking noise with his dentures. 'Who knows?' he said at last. 'Who knows what an angel would be doing in a century like this one? Maybe he was just meant to be an angel for our times.' There was a long pause. 'Immortal spirit burned in him, you see ... Sin meant nothing to him; he was pure soul. This was his tragedy.'

'His tragedy?'

Harry nodded. 'To be pure soul in an age that would not believe its existence.' He asked me to give him more gin. I was feeling very irritable as I poured his gin.

We sat there, Harry and I, in silence, he no doubt contemplating these spurious memories of his, while I wondered how soon I could decently escape. Harry had taken from his pocket a small jade compact and was powdering his face with rapid, jerky movements, his eyes averted from me so I had only the beaky profile. 'Pure soul,' he repeated, in a murmur, 'in an age that would not believe its existence.'

'What happened to him?' I said wearily.

'Oh,' he replied, snapping shut the compact, 'I lost sight of him. I believe he came to a bad end; I believe he was sent to prison.'

'No he wasn't.'

Harry looked at me sharply. There was, for the first time in our relationship, a genuinely honest contact between us. All the rest had been indulgence on his part and acquiescence 15 on mine. 'Am I so transparent?' he said. 'I suppose I must be. Dear Bernard, you're angry with me.'

I rose to my feet and moved to the window and stared into the night. 'I don't think Anson Havershaw ever existed,' I said. 'There was instead a man consumed with guilt who created a fairy story about angels and spirits in order to conceal certain truths from himself.' Why, I thought, do old drunks always choose me to tell their stories to?

'I haven't told you the complete truth,' said Harry.

'There was no Anson Havershaw,' I said.

'Oh there was, there was. There is,' said Harry. A pause. Then: 'There was no Harry Talboys.'

I turned. This I was not prepared for.

'I am Anson Havershaw.'

I laughed.

He nodded. 'I shall show you,' he said, and rising to his feet, he began laboriously to remove his jacket, and then to unbutton his shirt.

In the middle of Harry's ceiling was a fixture into which three light bulbs were screwed. A short length of chain hung from it; Harry pulled the chain, and the room was flooded with a harsh raw light. Beneath his shirt, it now became apparent, he wore a garment of some sort of off-white surgical plastic. Slowly he removed his shirt. The plastic, which was quite grubby, encased him like a sleeveless tunic from his upper chest to a line somewhere below the belt of his trousers. It was fastened down the side by a series of little buckles, and a very narrow fringe of dirty gauze peeped from the upper edge, where the skin was rubbed to an angry rash. Harry's arms were the arms of a very old man, the flesh hanging from the bone in loose white withered flaps. He smiled slightly, for I suppose I must have been gazing with horrified curiosity at this bizarre corset of his. I was standing close to the incense, and as Harry fumbled with the buckles I brought the censer up under my nose; for the smell rapidly became very bad indeed. He dropped his trousers and underpants. The corset extended to his lower belly, forming a line just above a hairless pubis and a tiny, uncircumcised penis all puckered up and wrinkled in upon itself. He loosed the final straps; holding the corset to his body with his fingers, he told me gently that I must not be shocked. And then he revealed himself to me.

There was, first of all, the smell; a wave of unspeakable foulness was released with the removal of the corset, and to defend my senses I was forced to clamp my nostrils and inhale the incense with my mouth. Harry's flesh had rotted off his lower ribs and belly, and the clotted skin still clinging to the ribs and hipbones that bordered the hole was in a state of gelatinous putrescence. In the hole I caught the faint gleam of his spine, and amid an indistinct bundle of piping the forms of shadowy organs. I saw sutures on his intestines, and the marks of neat stitching, and a cluster of discolored organic vessels bound with a thin strip of translucent plastic. He should have been dead, and I suppose I must have whispered as much, for I heard him say that he could not die. How long I stood there gazing into his decaying torso I do not know; at some point I seemed to become detached 17 from my own body and saw as if from high up and far away the two figures standing in the room, the flowers and the crucifix between them, myself clutching the censer and Harry standing with his opened body and his trousers at his ankles. It took long enough, I suppose, for the full horror of his condition to be borne home to me. This is what it means to be an angel, I remember thinking, in our times at least: eternal life burned in him while his body, his temple, crumbled about the flame. Out there in the hot night the city trembled with a febrile life of its own, and somewhere a siren leaped into sudden desolate pain. All I saw then was a young man standing in the corner of a shabby room watching an old man pull up his trousers.

As I write this it is late January, and very cold outside. Snow lies heaped in filthy piles along the edge of the sidewalk, and the Chrysler Building is a bleak gray needle against a thickening winter afternoon sky. The men from the men's shelter huddle in the doorways in the Bowery, selling cigarettes from off the tops of plastic milk crates, and the smell of incense still pervades the lower floors of the building. I can't help thinking of him as Harry – it seems somehow to suit him better. He asked me to write an account of our friendship, I wouldn't otherwise have done it; writing seems futile now. Everything seems futile, for some reason I don't fully understand, and I keep wondering why any of us cling to the raft. The one consolation I can find is the presence of that other spirit traveling with us in the body – a consolation denied my rotting friend downstairs, whoever, whatever, he is.

The Black Hand of the Raj

Nineteenth-century Imperialism, as Lenin understood it, appeared when the great European capitalists began to have difficulty finding sound investment opportunities for their superfluous wealth at home. They turned to Africa and the East, and backed by the armed might of the state and an ideology of racial superiority proceeded to expand. Expansion bred competition, and competition bred war. War, of course, breeds only death, and death breeds nothing except maybe flowers and vegetables, which are good only for antiquated agricultural economies. What this rather gloomy analysis tends to ignore, however, is Imperialism's other face, which is indeed more properly the preserve of fiction. This is the soft face of Imperialism, and it concerns itself with human relationships, and individual psychology – and not least with the education of the senses. For it was in the torrid climates of the various far-flung corners of the Empire that many Europeans first confronted the nature of passion. Frequently the experience proved liberating, and the traveler emerged from the glowing crucible a richer, wiser, and more fully rounded human being. But occasionally, the encounter of East and West, of the sensual and the rational, did not resolve so satisfactorily. Occasionally, darker forces seemed to be at work, forces committed to discord and antipathy between the races. The Black Hand of the Raj was one such force.

It is a warm night in the spring of 1897, and gazing at the stars from the upper deck of a P & O liner bound for Bombay stands a young woman named Lucy Hepplewhite. Her hands rest lightly upon the rough dark wood of the rail, and her face is bathed in moonlight. A soft breeze lifts the delicate tassels of the lace mantilla she has thrown about her shoulders, and gently ruffles the curls escaping from her piled tresses. Her dark eyes are misted and shining, and from between her soft lips small pearly teeth gleam like stars. But what is it that brings now a gentle smile to those ripe lips? What is she thinking of, this flower of Victorian maidenhood, as she turns her gaze to the gleaming surface of the darkly heaving waters below? She is thinking of the altar. She is thinking of love. For she is going to India to marry a young man in the Indian Civil Service to whom she became engaged some six months previously. His name is Cecil Pym, and he occupies an important post in Poonah. It is there that the happy couple will be married, and afterwards honeymoon elsewhere in the hill country. The prospect arouses in Lucy a strange excitement, a vague and delicious warmth that she is hesitant to define; then the sea breeze freshens and she turns, with a last glance at the moonlit swells, and goes below, leaving the deck deserted.

The voyage was uneventful for the most part, and Lucy amused herself with a little bridge, an occasional game of deck quoits, and pleasant expectations of connubial bliss with Cecil. The prospect of life in India had never unduly alarmed her; however, as the great vessel slipped down the Suez Canal, the weather grew uncomfortably warm and brought an immoderate flush to her pale cheek. She retired to her cabin and was troubled, for the first time in her life, by thoughts that were less than spotlessly pure. And in that moment the first faint whisper of a doubt as to how she would cope with the weather began to disturb her serenity.

But she did not brood upon the matter, for it was not in her nature to do so. She banished the shadow that had fallen briefly across her mind, and carried a parasol whenever she promenaded. And in the fullness of time the ship docked at Bombay, and Lucy Hepplewhite made her way gingerly down the gangway and into the arms of a tall young Englishman in a high white pith helmet and a cream-colored suit of fine Madras cotton with a pale thin stripe of eggshell blue.

Only one incident marred their happy reunion, and that was a one-handed leper who emerged from the milling dockside crowd and, grinning hideously, shoved his begging bowl in Lucy's face. Cecil saw him off quickly enough, and Lucy, who was a girl of pretty stout kidney, was not unduly distraught. Still, as they trotted toward the Empress Hotel in a tonga for tea, she could detect the telltale signs of a light perspiration breaking out beneath her cotton underclothing. She was frankly relieved when they finally escaped the blazing Bombay sun and found shelter in the cool depths of the Empress.

Lucy had heard that men changed after being in India for even a short while; and later that night, as she sat in Cecil's compartment on the train to Poonah, she asked herself if *he* had. The answer was, alas, yes. The spirited and carefree young man she'd known in England had become quiet, and rather inward. He seemed depressed. He rarely laughed, and often his eyes drifted off into the middle distance, and became clouded, as if with some private anguish. Whatever that anguish was, Lucy was resolved that once in Poonah, and the wedding behind them, she would soothe it with womanly balm and restore him to a state of untroubled happiness. And then another question popped into her mind.

'Cecil?'

'Darling?' He turned to her from the window, whence he had been gazing with a frown of perplexity into the hot living night of India.

'Why do you never take off your pith helmet?'

It was true. Ever since he'd met her at the docks the pith helmet had not once been doffed. Not that it didn't add a certain commanding elegance to his appearance – but the question seemed to disturb him. His jaw tightened and the finely chiseled nostrils quivered slightly.

'Must I?' he murmured. 'Now?'

And then, to Lucy's amazement, he pounded the door of the compartment with his fist and began sobbing uncontrollably!

'Darling!' she cried, gathering him into her arms. 'Cecil, what is it? Is it – too tight?' And she reached for the pith helmet.

'No!' He leaped away from her, clutching his headgear to his skull.

'Cecil, you must tell me,' whispered Lucy, gazing at him with distress and concern. It was a warm night, and she was beginning to feel damp again.

There was a long silence. The engine chuffed on through the darkness, and the rails chattered beneath them. Far off in the hills a wild dog began howling at the moon. Cecil was hunched forward in his seat, his elbows on his knees and his head in his hands. And then he turned toward her, and she saw that his face was haggard with pain.

'Very well,' he said quietly, 'I'll tell you.'

.

It was not a long story, nor was it a happy one. Lucy heard it through to the bitter end, defying convention by staying in Cecil's compartment through the hours of darkness. But they were, after all, soon to be married.

He first described to her a little ruined summerhouse in an overgrown garden not far from his bungalow in the British cantonment in Poonah. Long since abandoned to the monkeys and the insects, and colonized by luxuriant vines whose great drooping flowers emanated odors of incense and musk, it was yet a pleasant shady spot for a smoke after dinner, and Cecil had come to think of it as his own. And then one day he'd found a little old man with a bald bead and a loincloth meditating there. He'd scrounged a cigarette from Cecil and then blessed him by laying his hands on Cecil's head. Cecil had thought nothing of it at the time, but the next day he'd felt a slight irritation where the old man had touched him, and the day after that a small brown lump had appeared on his crown. Then the lump had started to grow, and it had been growing ever since. When Cecil went to the doctor – an old boy named Cadwallader, not up to much on account of pink gins – he'd been told to come back in a week.

'But after a week,' said Cecil – and then broke down for the second time. Again Lucy took him in her arms, and murmured words of comfort. Finally the young Englishman sat up straight, and pluckily unbuckled the thin leather strap fastened snugly beneath his chin.

In India, the appearance of a certain sort of plump and blustery raincloud is a sure sign that the monsoons are at hand. One such cloud drifted now across the moon and threw the swaying compartment into deep shadow. So it was that when Cecil slowly removed the pith helmet, Lucy was at first uncertain what exactly she was looking at. Her first thought was of a dark brown lily splayed limply from a short thick stem attached somehow to Cecil's skull; but how could that be? And then the raincloud drifted on and in the sudden glow of moon light she realized that the brown stem was in fact a *wrist*; that it was *growing* out of Cecil's head; and that the dark limp lily atop it was a *hand*!

For a dreadful moment all sympathy fled Lucy's heart, and she knew only horror. She stared aghast at the gruesome sprout, and her own hands flew to her mouth. Cecil watched her from hooded and anguished eyes. 'Now you see why I wear my pith helmet,' he said, and covered the alien extremity.

There was little left to tell. Once the hand had come through, it proved to be rather active, constantly pulling his hair and sticking its fingers in his ears. Dr Cadwallader had refused to amputate, saying it was connected to the brainstem, and instead prescribed a heavy sedative. Twice a day Cecil would have to inject a few cc into the thing's wrist to keep it quiet. 'In fact,' he said, glancing at his watch, 'it's about time. Darling, would you mind?'

And so, as the first pale streaks of dawn crept over the land, Lucy Hepplewhite assisted her fiancé in injecting a heavy dose of some powerful narcotic into the wrist growing out of the top of his head. It was not a pleasant task, and when it was all over she slumped into her seat, exhausted, while Cecil turned again to the window.

Once in Poonah, Lucy was dropped off at the Florence Nightingale Residence for Young Women, and she kissed Cecil fondly before he went on to his own bungalow. Deep shadows had appeared around the young man's eyes, and in the light of early morning a note of gaunt and terrible despair could be detected in his features. He seemed, again, broken and helpless before his grim fate, and Lucy's heart went out to him. 'Don't torment yourself, darling,' she whispered, laying her small white palm on his cheek. 'I'm here now.'

'But how can you love a man with a hand growing out of his head?' he whispered furiously.

'Trust me,' murmured Lucy; but she was never to see him alive again.

Lucy retired to her room at the residence and fell asleep almost immediately. Her dreams were less than tranquil, however; she tossed and turned beneath her mosquito net, and through the turbulent flood of images that coursed about her fevered mind, one reared up with greater frequency and intensity than all the others – and that was the hand growing out of Cecil's head. But in Lucy's dream it was not sedated – very far from it: it writhed and twisted and beckoned and pointed, it throbbed and undulated like a serpent, and performed gestures of an unspeakably lewd nature. Lucy awoke with a wild cry of panic, and the hand disappeared. But the sensation persisted, and she found she was perspiring heavily.

She arose, rather weakly, soon after, and bathed, unable to sleep more; and some hours later found her way across the cantonment to Cecil's bungalow. No servant answered the door, so she quietly let herself in. It was late afternoon now, and very still. She called Cecil's name; the sound died in the deep silence that lay upon the place like a pall, and the girl shivered. Shadows were beginning to gather in the corners of Cecil's neat and sparsely furnished sitting room. Beside a low couch upholstered in black leather a whisky bottle, a soda siphon, and a glass of cut crystal stood upon a small table. On one wall hung a sepia-toned photograph of Cecil at Oxford, and beside it her own image. She gazed at them wistfully. Would she ever see that smile of guileless charm upon the young man's face again? For a moment the dream returned, and a light flush crept over her cheeks.

'Cecil!' she called. 'Cecil!'

Still nothing; so she passed through the sitting room and into the hallway beyond, at the end of which stood a closed door. That, she guessed, was his bedroom; and then a

terrible feeling of nameless dread leaped up within her, and she resisted only with difficulty a fierce impulse to flee the place. Resolutely, though, she advanced, and now she thought she could hear something in the room beyond, a sort of furtive, muffled, slithering sound. A prickle of fear ran up Lucy Hepplewhite's spine, and a gust of adrenalin welled in her belly.

'Cecil!' she called again, walking unsteadily toward his bedroom.

The slithering sound had stopped, and Lucy's hand was upon the doorknob. She took a deep breath, then threw open the door – and such was the sight that met her eyes that a violent spasm seized her slight frame, and a scream died on her lips. For there on the floor by the unmade bed lay the half-naked body of Cecil Pym, his face purple, his eyes bulging, his tongue protruding grotesquely, and the heavy bruises of strangulation dark upon his sunburned neck! Beside him lay a hypodermic syringe, the plunger yet undepressed, and the third hand, still very much attached to the dead man's crown, lying palm down on the floor, the fingers slightly curled.

For some minutes Lucy stood there rigid with horror, and no sound escaped her. And then a choked sob finally burst free and she flung herself on him. 'Oh, Cecil,' she whimpered, clinging to his still-warm body, 'who has done this thing to you?' She touched him with frantic fingers, searching for life, but there was none. How long she lay there as the shadows gathered about her and the insects began their shrill and rasping chorus in the dusk, she would never know. But suddenly she became aware that her hair was being very gently stroked.

'Cecil,' she murmured. 'Cecil, are you still with me?'

And in a way he was; for the dark hand growing out of his head had begun to softly caress Lucy's hair. And such was the lightness, the delicacy of its touch, that the demented girl did not recoil in horror, but remained, sobbing, on the corpse, as the hand soothed her and calmed her and brought her slowly to a state of passive languor; and when it gently touched her neck she still did not resist, did not leap back in disgust, but allowed the fingers to melt her pain to pleasure and revive the longings that had first been spawned by the hot sun of Suez; and once again Lucy Hepplewhite was filmed with perspiration, and she moaned in the shadows of the body of her lover.

When she arose from the body an hour later, her cotton underclothing was in a state of disarray and two red stains of shame burned upon her cheeks. Her hair was damply plastered to her brow, and a deep tranquility smoldered in her drowsy eyes. The hand lay still and quiet now, palm upwards, and Cecil was beginning to go bad. So without further ado Lucy adjusted her dress, tidied her hair, and washed her face in a basin of cold water. And then she went to look for Dr Cadwallader.

'Bad business,' muttered the portly and florid physician, standing over the body and reeking of gin. He shook his head as the servants placed Cecil's three-handed corpse on to a stretcher and covered it with a white sheet. 'Black Hand of the Raj,' he said, turning to Lucy, who was sniffling quietly into a lace handkerchief. 'Always fatal. Couldn't tell him that, of course.'

'You mean it's happened before?' said Lucy, glancing up sharply.

''Fraid so,' said Cadwallader. 'Lost a number of good men this way. Never can find the little fellow in the loincloth. Some sort of wog curse, I suppose.' And he put his plump fingers to his throat, as if to demonstrate. It was at that precise moment that Lucy finally succumbed to stress, and fainted, and was revived only with great difficulty, a heavy dose of smelling salts, and a small glass of brandy from a bottle which the doctor happened to be carrying in his black bag.

India being rather a warm country, it was necessary to bury Cecil Pym the very next day. Happily, he did not take the black hand with him to the grave: Cadwallader severed it with a surgical saw and a couple of sharp knives, pickled it in vinegar, and deposited the jar in a cupboard with a number of other carefully labeled specimens. The funeral went off smoothly enough, as these things go. Lucy, veiled and lovely in black crêpe de chine, hung grieving on the porky arm of the doctor throughout, and the sun beat down on the small group of late-Victorian colonials with an intense and unrelenting ferocity. It was only when the minister began to pray for the deceased that she looked up, disturbed by Cadwallader's reaching to remove his hat. And as her damp eye blearily scanned the mourners at the graveside, it was with a ghastly tremor of foreboding that she counted no fewer than seven Englishmen conspicuous for not having removed their headgear – and the Deputy Commissioner was among them!

After the funeral Lucy did not linger long in Poonah, nor indeed in India. Within a week she had boarded a ship for home. The Lucy who left Bombay, however, was a very different creature from the one who had arrived there mere days before. She played no bridge now, and could not be tempted to deck quoits. Instead, she leaned on the rail, still in black, gazing out to sea. And by the time she was under an English heaven once more, she had reached her decision.

•

Twenty-five years ago today an old nun was buried in the graveyard of a small convent in Tunbridge Wells. Her name was Mother Constance, but we know her better as Lucy Hepplewhite. Yes, she had joined the Sisters of Perpetual Atonement and lived out her days behind the cloister walls. She took no interest in the great events that rocked the subcontinent in the half-century or so after her departure. Instead, she became a model of piety and self-sacrifice, offering prayers without stint for the soul of poor dead Cecil Pym, and wondering, in her heart of hearts, what, exactly, was the nature of the sin she had committed.

The Arnold Crombeck Story

One of the most memorable events of my long journalistic career was the series of interviews I conducted with Arnold Crombeck, the infamous 'death gardener' of Wimbledon, England, shortly before he was hanged in the summer of 1954. I was a young woman then, fresh from Vassar, and I'd been sent over by a big New York daily to cover the tennis. Sportswriting held little interest for me in 1954, and it holds even less today, so when a call came into the office from Mr Crombeck's lawyer saying that his client was eager to meet with the American press, I quickly volunteered for the assignment. Crombeck's appeal had already been turned down, and his execution was fixed for the morning of July 17 – less than two weeks away.

Now, a woman reporter really had to prove herself in those days, otherwise all she'd get to write about was fashion and tennis. I was ambitious; I was eager to show that I could handle hard news as well as any man – this was why I'd jumped at the Arnold Crombeck story. But how to approach it? I decided that the human-interest angle was the one to go for here. Accordingly, I became curious about the state of mind of a man who, having murdered quite promiscuously for a number of years, was about to find himself on the receiving end. What must it feel like? I asked myself. I thought the folks back home might be curious too, if I served it up the right way. And so, armed with pencils and notebooks and cigarettes and questions, I made my way to Wandsworth.

This is one of the big London prisons, built like a fortress, and you feel nervous about going in; you can't help thinking they might not let you out again. They were quite gruff with me. No institution likes the press inside its walls, and to make matters very much worse, I was a woman, and an American. But the paperwork was in order, and in due time I was cleared. A dour man in a black uniform and black peaked cap led me off through the prison on what seemed an interminable journey, broken every few yards by locked doors. At last we reached a visitors' room with a tiled floor and a small barred window set high in the wall. There was a stout wooden table scarred with cigarette burns, and a chair on either side of it; nothing else. There I was told to wait.

I laid my notebook on the table. I lit a Chesterfield and watched the smoke swirling through the bars of bright sunshine that came streaming through the window. The room was painted a drab green to within a few feet of the ceiling, at which point it unaccountably turned off-beige. A twisted flypaper dangled from the electrical cord; it was black with insects, many of them still struggling in their last agonies. Then the door clanged open, and I was in the presence of the 'death gardener' himself.

Arnold Crombeck was a small man, bald, and wearing round, horn-rimmed spectacles. His prison clothes – gray shirt, gray trousers – were immaculately clean, and freshly pressed. The man himself wore an expression I can only describe as 'owlish'. He peered at me with an intensely eager expression, then advanced smartly across the room, shook my hand, and sat down. The guard took up his position with his back to the door, and fixed his eyes on a point high on the opposite wall.

Now, I hadn't as yet decided quite how I should present Arnold Crombeck to the American public. I thought, if I start by telling them everything he's *done*, then they'll see only the monster, and not the man. But if I show the man first, and then tell them what he's done – well, that's altogether the more interesting approach. So I took careful note of my first impressions.

I suppose I'd expected that someone capable of the crimes Arnold Crombeck had committed would be coarse and stupid. I was surprised, then, to find not only that this little man could speak with wit and erudition on a wide range of topics, but that he had made precisely the same assumptions about me – simply because I was American! That first meeting, then, was one in which we quietly corrected each other's preconceptions.

I asked him how he found prison life. Quite tolerable, he told me; he'd always been a voracious reader, he said, and they'd allowed him some of his books. His only complaint was that there were no plants. He was, he said, with no trace of irony, a keen amateur gardener, and not to have green, growing things around him was torture. They wouldn't even let him have a vase of flowers. This struck him as a pretty callous piece of bureaucratic indifference. He *was* going to be hanged, after all; he *was* going to pay his debt. Why, then, he should be deprived of the comfort of a few green things in his last hours he failed to understand. 'A bunch of lupins would brighten the cell nicely,' he said.

He then asked me where I was from, and on hearing the word *California* he became quite excited. He was familiar with newspaper accounts of the last hanging carried out in San Quentin, and they apparently confirmed that Americans were no good at hanging people. It was just as well, he said, that 'you've gone in for gas chambers and electric chairs instead'. He himself was fortunate in that he was going to be hanged by the English method, and in an English prison. All this he told me with a bright smile, his spotlessly clean hands laid flat on the table. There's an *art* to hanging people, he told me. You have to watch for two things: (a) – and here he placed the tip of one index finger on the tip of the other – that death comes instantaneously; and (b) – index on middle finger – that it leaves as few marks on the body as possible. 'You people could never manage it,' he said. 'You always tore the bloke's head off. I've read Mencken on the subject. Know your problem?'

I didn't.

'Bad noose. For a quick, clean hang, what you want is not the old "hangman's knot". We don't use it.'

'No?'

'Running noose,' he said. 'Absolutely essential. A metal ring is woven into one end of the rope.' He made of his thumb and index finger a circle. 'The other end is passed through to form the loop. Makes for a faster drop, you see. The ring is placed under the angle of the left jaw' – he indicated the place on his own jaw – 'so the chin tilts back, and the spinal cord' – he put his fingers on the back of his neck – 'is ruptured between the second and fifth cervical vertebrae. Death' – he snapped his fingers – 'is instantaneous. No blood to the brain, you see.' He looked at me expectantly, as if to say, even an American can appreciate *that*, surely.

All this, he said, would happen to him next week. He'd be taken into the shed and stood over the drop. He planned to refuse the cap. 'A lever is pulled,' he said. 'The bolts slide back, the trapdoors fall – and down I go! Then, with a crisp *snap!*, my descent is arrested forever. The whole thing,' he added, 'should take about fifteen seconds, handled competently.'

It was hard to know quite what to say. But Arnold had not finished. After *that*, he said, his heart would maintain a gradually diminishing beating for perhaps ten or twelve minutes. 'My legs will draw up a bit,' he said, 'but not violently. I hope to God there'll be no urine spilled, and no seminal emission. Above all' – he grinned at me – 'no erection. I have to be buried in these trousers!'

I grinned back, rather weakly. 'The prospect of dying doesn't alarm you?' I managed to say.

'Dying? Good Lord no.' He shook his head. 'I deserve it, oh, I richly deserve it. I'm Arnold Crombeck, after all,' he said, with a twinkle. 'I'm the mild-mannered monster of Wimbledon!'

At this he rose and gave me his hand. 'Miss Kennedy, it's been a pleasure,' he said. 'Perhaps we can talk again in a few days?'

I said that would be fine.

'Good. Shall we say Friday, then? Same time?'

I left Wandsworth in a state of mild shock. Nothing had prepared me for the sprightly charm of this macabre little man. I found it necessary to reread the newspaper accounts of the trial, just to remind myself that I was dealing with a cold-blooded killer, a psychopathic personality, a man said to be brutal, remote, and indifferent to the plight of others. I found myself dreading the next meeting, but at the same time looking forward to it with a perverse sort of fascination. It was with a particularly delicious thrill of horror that I remembered his concern about the state of his trousers in the immediate aftermath of his execution. The man was vain about his own corpse!

There was, I remember, some kidding at the office, not all of it good-natured, about my Arnold Crombeck story. Some of the men were disturbed that I wasn't sticking to fashion and tennis. I realized then that it was crucial that I see this one through, and make a good job if it. Fortunately, my editor was supportive. After I'd filed the first installment he told me that the response had been good. There was plenty of space that summer, he said, for a grisly yarn about a loony Limey. I returned to Wandsworth on Friday feeling briskly optimistic.

And once again I had to wait in the front office for forty-five minutes for clearance; and then the long trek down corridors and stairwells, with a silent, disapproving man in a black uniform beside me, the whole grim trip punctuated by the jangle of big keys, the opening and closing of thick doors, and the intense stares of the men we passed – men who looked as if they hadn't seen a woman in ten years, and probably most of them hadn't. And so to that dingy little visitors' room at the heart of the prison, with its gently twisting flypaper and its bars of hot, bright sunshine.

Arnold was, again, crisp and alert. He seemed delighted to see me. His eyes gleamed behind his spectacles, and he sat down, as before, with his hands laid flat on the table and his cigarettes and matches between them, lined up perfectly perpendicular to the edge of the table.

'How did you feel, Mr Crombeck,' I began, 'when the police caught you?'

And then something rather dreadful happened. All the pleasure drained from Arnold's face. The gleam in his eye turned glassy. He said, in a very icy voice: 'The police did not catch me, Miss Kennedy. I thought you were familiar with my case.'

He watched me carefully. The man at the door quietly cleared his throat, and shifted his weight from foot to foot. Did this mean something?

'Forgive me, Mr Crombeck. Let me rephrase my question. Would you describe for my readers the circumstances of your arrest?' Christ, I thought, I have to flatter the little bastard!

He appeared somewhat mollified, but the original warmth was gone. He asked me, rather sardonically, if I knew how many murders he'd committed. I gave him the figure I'd read in the English papers. He said it was imprecise, but that it would do. He then pursued a rather horrible train of thought for some minutes, elaborating on the idea of murder as one of the fine arts. Apparently the notion was not original 37 with him; Thomas De Quincey, the opium eater, had articulated it a hundred years before. Then he described to me in detail the sensations that accompany the act of murder, and by this time I knew that he was simply trying to revolt me. He was succeeding, too, but I was damned if I'd show it. His tone, throughout, was bitterly sarcastic, and I was furious with myself for having lost his sympathy. I kept forgetting that I was dealing – as he himself had admitted – with a monster!

Well, he came to believe, he said, that his 'oeuvre' was complete – 'adequate for posterity', as he put it – and so he invited the police to 'admire his garden'. He finished up with an account of his arrest. He stressed the quiet and orderly manner in which it was conducted. He praised the British police force. 'I expect if it had happened in your country,' he said drily, 'I'd have gone down in a hail of bullets, wouldn't I? The idea is most unattractive. And I don't think I'd want to be hanged in America, either, Miss Kennedy. Or gassed. Or electrified. No, a short drop on a running noose, then – snap!' He snapped his fingers. 'That will suit me nicely. Have a cigarette.'

I took a cigarette. I needed it. For some moments Arnold smoked in silence, while I scribbled in my pad. I suddenly noticed how many flies were buzzing about the ceiling of that hot little room; and then I became aware that Arnold was smiling at me! The bile had drained off, he was happy once more, he was smiling at me! 'Gardens,' he said softly. 'We must talk about gardens, Miss Kennedy.'

And then, indeed, we talked about gardens – or rather, *he*

talked about gardens, he talked about nature, and I glimpsed the delicate flame of humanity that yet flickered in his heart. I did not take notes, and only later reconstructed his general drift. 'When I speak of *my* garden,' he said, 'I do not mean the Wimbledon garden, Miss Kennedy. That was a fairly modest affair, but I left it a better garden than I found it, which is something to be proud of . . . I grew some lovely flowers in that soil . . . No, when I speak of *my* garden, I have in mind the *ideal* garden. Do you believe in God, Miss Kennedy? Well, imagine God Almighty suddenly saying to you: "You may have any garden on earth, Miss Kennedy." What would you choose? I know what I would choose. I would choose an English country garden. Without a moment's hesitation.'

Arnold's eyes were bright. He went on to describe the clipped hedges this God-given garden of his would have, the shady, graveled walks, the bower thick with crimson rambler where he would sit and read on summer days. There would be a pond, he said, in the shade of a weeping willow tree, where goldfish darted among the stems of water lilies, and insects drifted across the glinting and shadow-dappled surface; and set against a dark box hedge nearby, garden figures of nymphs, and sylphs, and goddesses, all in stone . . . He described in loving detail these stone figures, then paused and gazed at me, his head craning forward and his face glowing, though his hands were, as ever, flat and still upon the table. 'The lawn is as smooth as velvet, Miss Kennedy, and the flowers – the flowers! – my garden is ablaze all summer, Miss Kennedy, with sweet William, with irises and 39

peonies, with carnations, wallflowers, and Canterbury
bells! . . .'

I left Wandsworth emotionally exhausted. Time spent in
Arnold's company allowed for no relaxation, no ease. He
engaged one, at every moment. It was extraordinarily stimulat-
ing; it was also extraordinarily debilitating. I went back to
my hotel and took a hot bath, feeling weak and somewhat
queasy. That night I vomited violently for the first time since
I was a little girl, and I had bad diarrhea too. Nevertheless, I
went into the office the next day and filed my story. I was
pale and unsteady, and in no mood for the gibes of the men.
I was to see Arnold once more, on the following Tuesday.
Two days after that he would hang.

I did not spend a happy weekend. I read over my notes
and prepared for Tuesday. I would, I decided, write one
more piece on Arnold Crombeck the man – build it around
his country-garden fantasy, maybe – and then I'd reveal the
monster. But it seemed that even thinking about such things
was enough to make me ill, for I spent most of the next three
days with one end of me or the other stuck in the toilet bowl.
I presumed it was English cooking – one of their bloody pork
pies or something.

I felt slightly better on Tuesday, but still far from confident. I doubt I'd have felt confident even if I'd been in top
form – for in this, the last interview, I planned to ask Arnold
about his crimes, about all the women he'd murdered. But as
I was once again led down those grim, clanging corridors, I
found myself thinking not about his victims, not about all
those poor women, but about the man himself. Did death

really hold no terrors for him? For now – the chilling thought kept coming back to me – he had less than forty-eight hours to live!

But Arnold's composure was, as ever, perfect. The question intrigues me still, whether Arnold Crombeck was truly unconcerned about his imminent death, or simply assuming a mask. Was it all a *performance*? I still wonder. And I think, in the light of what I've learned about the human condition over the course of a long and distinguished journalistic career, that it *was* a performance. I think Arnold Crombeck was deeply terrified of being hanged – that was why he spoke of it in such obsessive detail. I think that the habit of self-restraint, of formality, was so deeply ingrained in him that he could not express his feelings even *in extremis*. And he *did* have feelings; there *was* a man inside the monster – of that I am certain. In the end one cannot but admire his control; it's very typically Anglo-Saxon, of course, though I wasn't mature enough to realize it at the time.

His composure was, as I say, perfect; but after a moment he said: 'Miss Kennedy, you don't look at all well.'

It was nothing, I told him; an upset stomach, no more. But he was very concerned, and offered to postpone the interview, although, as he said with a small smile, his schedule was 'rather tight' the next day or so, and after that – 'how would you put it, Miss Kennedy? I shall be out of town. Indefinitely!'

But I wouldn't hear of it, and after further assurances that I was quite well enough to continue, I broached my question. Arnold got the point immediately. 'Ah,' he said. 'Methodology.' 41

He was then silent for a moment, apparently gathering his thoughts. All was as usual – the guard at the door, the flies, the heat. It was a very hot summer, 1954, by British standards. Then he spoke.

'I have always been a neat man,' he said slowly. 'I was taught the importance of good tailoring early in life . . . Do you know Max Beerbohm, Miss Kennedy? A fine stylist; you would do well to study his constructions. Max says: "The first aim of modern dandyism is the production of the supreme effect through means the least extravagant." The same, I think, is true of murder.'

Like a preacher, Arnold proceeded to develop his text. I was not feeling at all well, and the content of Arnold's 'sermon' did little to improve matters. Nevertheless, I scribbled dutifully, mindlessly, as he spoke of his distaste for certain 'techniques'. 'Who can take pleasure in an ax murder, after all?' he said. 'Can you imagine the *mess*, Miss Kennedy?'

'Some murders are better than others, then?'

'Oh, good Lord, of course they are.'

'Such as?'

'Well, I have more respect for a drowner,' he said. 'Have you heard of G.J. Smith?'

I had not.

'Brides-in-the-bath man. True monster. Grew careless toward the end of his career; hanged at Maidstone in the summer of 1915. He didn't die well.' Arnold shook his head. 'Have to die well,' he murmured, drumming his fingers on the table – the first and only manifestation of anxiety I ever saw in the man. 'I've drowned,' he went on. 'Never from choice, always out of necessity. There's an art to it; there's a right way and a wrong way, as in everything else . . . But you know *my* method, don't you, Miss Kennedy?' The eyes gleamed behind the spectacles; the hands were flat on the table once more.

'You're a poisoner.'

'Precisely. And it's as a poisoner that I hope to be remembered.' He became very matter-of-fact at this point, very formal. 'I only poisoned women, Miss Kennedy, and I poisoned them three at a time.' He waited till I'd got that down. He seemed concerned that this segment of the interview be accurately recorded. 'Do you know what I would do with them then?'

'Tell me,' I said. I had read the papers, of course, but I wanted to get it straight from the horse's mouth, as it were.

'I posed them.'

'You posed them.'

'That's right. Have a cigarette, Miss Kennedy. I grouped them and draped them. I *arranged* them. I derived genuine aesthetic pleasure from it.'

'This was after –?'

'After they'd died, yes. I came to think of them as *tableaux morts*.'

He had to spell that one out for me.

'And it always seemed such a pity to have to dismantle them when the sun went down. But one day it occurred to me that I didn't have to.'

'Didn't have to what, Mr Crombeck?' My mouth was dry   43

as a bone, and my head was spinning. I could barely see the pad in front of me.

'Didn't have to dismantle them, Miss Kennedy. Not immediately, at any rate. I could keep them around for a few days, cohabit with them. And you know what I found?'

'No.'

'I found I could sleep like a baby with dead women in the house. You obviously don't suffer from insomnia, Miss Kennedy, so you won't understand what this means.'

'And then?' I was close to blacking out.

'Oh,' he said, 'then I planted them. Put them in the garden.'

'I see.'

'Got all that, Miss Kennedy?'

I had.

'Strange bird, the mind, eh?'

Well, that was the heart of darkness as far as Arnold Crombeck was concerned. He was willing, he told me, to go into greater detail if I wished; but that was quite enough for me. He seemed pleased. He terminated the interview shortly afterward. He shook my hand warmly and said he hoped I'd be feeling better soon. Then he nodded to the guard, and left the room. And that was the end of our relationship – or so I thought.

When I got back to the hotel I went straight to bed – and stayed there, apart from trips to the bathroom, for the next two days. I was really very ill, but I thought that I'd merely 'eaten something', and didn't call a doctor. On Thursday morning I listened to the BBC news. A crowd of at least two hundred people, most of them women and children, had gathered outside the gates of Wandsworth Prison, and at shortly after eight o'clock, when the black flag was run up, cheering broke out and lasted for ten minutes. Poor Arnold.

Half an hour later, I received a call from Scotland Yard. They told me not to go anywhere, and that an ambulance was on its way; and within a few minutes I was being wheeled out of the hotel, with a doctor in close attendance. I don't remember much about all this, quite frankly; I was very weak. When I was fully conscious again, I found myself propped up in a hospital bed. I'd had all my blood changed, they told me, a total transfusion.

'But why?'

They gave me a letter which, they said, had been found in Arnold Crombeck's cell shortly after he was hanged. I opened it with trembling fingers.

'Dear Miss Kennedy,' it began, in beautiful copperplate script. 'If you are able to read this, then I must apologize for causing you so much unpleasantness. I did enjoy our talks, but I'm afraid I couldn't resist the temptation to try just one more; one for the road, as we say. I've always wanted to murder an American, so when they sent you along, and you were *female* to boot – well, I indulged myself, I'm afraid.

'Doubtless you're wondering how I managed it. It was not complicated. One flypaper soaked in water for twenty-four hours produces enough arsenic in solution to poison any normal person. Simple enough matter then to transfer it to cigarettes. But you know, the effectiveness of any poison depends to a large extent on the constitution of the victim, and if you can read this then I congratulate you. I've always heard you were a robust people . . .

[There followed several paragraphs that concern only Arnold and me.]

'I have very little time left, so I must close. Don't forget me, Miss Kennedy; and pray God I don't ruin these trousers, for as you know, I should hate to be planted not looking my best.

'Yours faithfully,
'Arnold Crombeck.'

I still have that letter, and I certainly never did forget him. And as for his trousers, I contacted the prison authorities as soon as I got out of the hospital, and learned that for once Arnold had got his facts wrong. Executed convicts are buried within the prison walls, in a lime pit – stark naked. But if he *had* been buried in his trousers –? I asked them. And you can rest assured, Arnold, wherever you are, that your trousers were spotless to the end.

The E(rot)ic Potato

I am a fly called Gilbert and I live by a pond, a stagnant
pond in a bird sanctuary. The surface of the pond is covered
by a carpet of tiny bright green organic discs. The reeds and
the rushes still thrust up from the muddy bed below, and as
the breeze plays over the water the leafy tendrils of a weeping
willow on the bank stir gently. Climb the bank and you will
find, set back in the trees, a tumbledown shed. This is where
the E(ROT)IC POTATO is.

One day I flew up the bank where the shadows hang and
the ivy claws at the gray stones edging flatly out of the
irradiated earth. Forms of other insects flashed by me. I
settled upon a branch and turned my compound eyes toward
the shed which housed the E(ROT)IC POTATO. It lay
beneath the trees, and though its windows were smashed and
boarded up with cardboard, its roof was whole. The white
paint was peeling off the boards, and the door was held
closed by a rusty nail. One hinge hung loose. The sharp
tap of a bird's beak rattled suddenly through the air. A
butterfly emerged from between the cardboard and the shattered windowpane. A rusting tool, half in sunlight and half in
shadow, was leaned against the wall beside the shaky door. I
did not go further. I knew I would be turned back. I was not
yet ready to enter the presence of the E(ROT)IC
POTATO. The emergent butterfly drifted by me in the

dappled woodland sunlight, and I returned to the pond.

On the way I found a fairly large crowd of insects gathered round a poisoned water rat, and the air was abuzz with the vibrations of fine wings and the chatter of excited voices. The creature lay on the bank shivering, for its pelt had lost the sleek oily texture that insulated the mammal within. After a few feeble attempts to haul its body up the bank it collapsed limply and lay panting, near death, in the mud. A yellow fluid seeped thickly from its ears and eyes, and a greenish discoloration spread across its soft underbelly. As the breathing grew heavier, the mouth opened and sucked air and we saw that its teeth had crumbled to impotent stumps. A rat without teeth was doomed, in our world.

Several flies and some ants had already mounted the body and were sampling tissue. They quickly discovered that the irradiation was mild, and once again we were confronted by proof of our biological superiority: that rat couldn't breathe our air and live. A warm pulse ran through the crowd, and then we set to.

There was more than enough for all, but naturally we wanted to lay open the belly first and get at the inner organs. The biters and chewers were quickly ushered to the front, and went to work. The rest of us buzzed about, making inroads where we could. I was set to breaking down blockage in the left ear, to clear a passage to the brain.

Some time later word spread that the ants had got through, and we buzzed down to have a look. Ariadne the dragonfly had been flitting about the head for a while, and flew close to me on the short hop to the opened belly. I was thrilled by her proximity, and though our eyes did not meet I knew she was aware of me.

There was a buzzy crunch on the belly of the water rat, and in all the confusion of eager mandibles and flashing wings my body drew very close to Ariadne's. I felt a tremor run through her as my proboscis glanced against her articulated thorax, and then something rather wonderful happened. Ariadne fluttered aloft and, hovering close, delicately displayed the milkwhite tip of her ovipositor to me. I was flooded by an irresistible genetic impulse to penetrate and fertilize her, but the trembling organ was withdrawn and the flashing blue-green dragonfly fluttered away.

Then, before my reeling senses could recover, they were again bombarded, this time by a meaty waft of warm fresh mammalian intestine. At that point I lost control completely and plunged into the innards of the rat's body with my fellows and fed.

The meal continued as the sun moved across an intensely brown sky. In the late afternoon, when the pond lay in shadow and nothing stirred the reeds, and the dripping tendrils of the weeping willow ululated imperceptibly and the tranquility was broken only by the endless declamations of the throstle-throated birds, and the countless tiny bright green organic discs had silently meshed to form an unbroken slimy weave over the poisoned water, the crab arrived.

'My turn, I think,' he murmured as he eased his great plated frame sideways up the bank. There was a din of protest at this, but the crustacean could not have cared less for the shrill outrage of a fly. He thrust a massive claw into the cadaver; and then, in full view of the assembled insects, he scooped out and consumed a dripping, glistening mountain of our eggs! The uproar intensified, but with utter indifference the hoary old scavenger shuffled his cantankerous and exoskeletal self entirely inside the rat's body, and within a few moments a steady, muffled grumble, basso profundo, was all that could be heard. He emerged, some time later, eructating, and made his way sideways back to the pond.

That night Ariadne admitted me to the E(ROT)IC POTATO. In a darkness strangely alive we flew from the body of the dead rat up the bank and through the trees to the shed. A full moon, tinted with toxins to the color of a rotting orange, bathed our rickety little temple in the febrile glow of post-apocalyptic romance. Ariadne's articulated rear segment trailed through the moonbeams and I flew steadily in her wake, inhaling drunkenly the subtle wisplets of insect love juice she was secreting. She landed with grace upon the edge of the windowframe and I came down beside her a moment later, swooning foolishly, barely conscious.

There were wasps everywhere. They swarmed about the shattered windowframe and squeezed themselves between the shards and the cardboard in the moonlight. Ariadne, her long smooth gauzy wings folded perpendicular above herself, twitched her slender tail sharply as one of these guardians approached us. I knew enough to let her do the talking.

'Good evening,' said the wasp smoothly.

Ariadne, rubbing her gossamer wings one against the other

and filling the air with a silky rustle that excited me beyond words, graced the handsome big stinger with a dazzling multifaceted glance.

'Ariadne,' said the wasp, with pleasure. 'And – a small fly?' I blew out my bulbous thorax, somewhat pricked by his tone.

'Roger, isn't it?' murmured Ariadne, and as the wasp inclined his head with slight irony, she went on briskly, 'Yes, I shall be taking him in with me.'

Then she rose into the air and hovered there, flicking her tail. 'No problem, is there, Roger?' she breathed, glancing down at the wasp.

'None at all,' he said, and with a small smile playing about his segmented lower mouthpart, he ushered her through the broken windowpane. I prepared to follow.

'Out late, little fly,' remarked the wasp. 'Fancied a bit of dragonfly, did we?'

The way he pronounced the word *dragonfly* left me in no doubt as to his meaning. It was a scurrilous imputation – so I buzzed him.

'Brat!' hissed the enraged yellow jacket, his sting-charged rear end whipping upward like a scorpion's. I zipped at high speed through the laser-thin gap between the shards and the cardboard and swept abuzzing into the temple of the E(ROT)IC POTATO.

And was immediately stopped short in my trajectory by the sheer majesty of the spectacle that lay before me. Ariadne hovered near a moonlit rafter and, wordlessly stupefied, thrilled beyond language, I joined her. Together we gazed down from the high regions of its cathedral upon the splendor of the E(ROT)IC POTATO.

It was a dead man lying on his back under a table, with one hand on his breast and the other on a book on the floor. His chest had caved in and the hand itself had flopped limply into the cavity where once had been the heart. The heart itself, of course, was long since devoured.

And the man's eyes and ears and mouth and belly were alive with insects! And the space between his body and the table was filled with flying insects! And their sounds were amplified by the gabled roof and filled the gloomy chamber like the very drone of Eternity itself! And that vast booming buzzing harmony was a sonic articulation of the Triumph of the Insectile Will!

'Come, Gilbert,' whispered Ariadne, and I followed her through the shafts of orange moonlight and descended with reverence deep into the bowels of the E(ROT)IC POTATO. There, in the darkness, I observed once again the milkwhite miracle of her ovipositor; but this time the organ was not withdrawn.

And then every dawning genetic tremor I had ever felt was finally fulfilled, not once, not twice, but a thousand times! A million times! A thousand million times! I quivered to the very quick of my being; I surrendered, fragmented, melted in the molten intolerable pleasure of it and dissolved to pure nonbeing, wrapped in shattering slithering Ariadne and sinking deeper and ever deeper into the glow and pulse of the degenerating intestine of the E(ROT)IC POTATO.

•

Later, still intoxicated, I lurched out, creamed and filmed with the eggy juices of insect love, and crawled away to lick my wings. The dull buzz of Eternity roared warmly through my drained and sated body, and I knew I was changed forever. As the moon sank to the horizon and the first brown rays of a new day probed the eastern sky, I knew I had finally become a fly.

PENGUIN 60s

MARTIN AMIS · *God's Dice*

HANS CHRISTIAN ANDERSEN · *The Emperor's New Clothes*

MARCUS AURELIUS · *Meditations*

JAMES BALDWIN · *Sonny's Blues*

AMBROSE BIERCE · *An Occurrence at Owl Creek Bridge*

DIRK BOGARDE · *From Le Pigeonnier*

WILLIAM BOYD · *Killing Lizards*

POPPY Z. BRITE · *His Mouth will Taste of Wormwood*

ITALO CALVINO · *Ten Italian Folktales*

ALBERT CAMUS · *Summer*

TRUMAN CAPOTE · *First and Last*

RAYMOND CHANDLER · *Goldfish*

ANTON CHEKHOV · *The Black Monk*

ROALD DAHL · *Lamb to the Slaughter*

ELIZABETH DAVID · *I'll be with You in the Squeezing of a Lemon*

N. J. DAWOOD (TRANS.) · *The Seven Voyages of Sindbad the Sailor*

ISAK DINESEN · *The Dreaming Child*

SIR ARTHUR CONAN DOYLE · *The Man with the Twisted Lip*

DICK FRANCIS · *Racing Classics*

SIGMUND FREUD · *Five Lectures on Psycho-Analysis*

KAHLIL GIBRAN · *Prophet, Madman, Wanderer*

STEPHEN JAY GOULD · *Adam's Navel*

ALASDAIR GRAY · *Five Letters from an Eastern Empire*

GRAHAM GREENE · *Under the Garden*

JAMES HERRIOT · *Seven Yorkshire Tales*

PATRICIA HIGHSMITH · *Little Tales of Misogyny*

M. R. JAMES AND R. L. STEVENSON · *The Haunted Dolls' House*

RUDYARD KIPLING · *Baa Baa, Black Sheep*

PENELOPE LIVELY · *A Long Night at Abu Simbel*

KATHERINE MANSFIELD · *The Escape*

READ MORE IN PENGUIN